Weava the Wilful Witch

Weava the Wilful Witch

Tiffany Mandrake

Illustrated by Martin Chatterton

www.littleharebooks.com

Little Hare Books
an imprint of
Hardie Grant Egmont
85 High Street
Prahran, Victoria 3181, Australia

www.littleharebooks.com

National Library of Australia
Cataloguing-in-Publication entry

Mandrake, Tiffany.

Weava the wilful witch / by Tiffany Mandrake;
illustrated by Martin Chatterton.

1st

978 1 921714 0 23 (pbk.)

Mandrake, Tiffany. Little horrors ; no. 6.

For primary school age.

Witches—Juvenile fiction.

Chatterton, Martin.

A823.3

Cover design by Martin Chatterton
Set in 16/22 pt Bembo by Clinton Ellicott
Printed by Griffin Press
Printed in Adelaide, Australia, January 2010

5 4 3 2 1

This product conforms to CPSIA 2008

Contents

For all you little horrors out there!
(You know who you are . . .)

—TM

To Libby Volke: after six books it's about
time you got an honourable mention

—MC

A Note from Tiffany Mandrake

Psst, this is me, Tiffany Mandrake, speaking to you from my cosy, creepy cottage in the grounds of Hag's Abademy of Badness. The Abademy is a place where bad fairies go to study how to be truly bad. It's not far from where you live, but you probably won't see it. The fairy-breed use special spells to make sure you don't.

It is run by three water hags, Maggie Nabbie, Auld Anni and Kirsty Breeks.

The hags started the Abademy because too many fairies were doing sweet deeds.

Sweet deeds are not always good deeds, and the world needs a bit of honest badness for balance. Otherwise, we humans get slack and lazy. The Abademy provides that balance. To enter the Abademy, young fairies must earn a Badge of Badness.

This is the story of Weava Charm, a wilful witchling who was determined to win her Badge of Badness, despite her sister's best efforts to stop her.

I don't come into this story at all, but the kit-fae told me about the problems Weava had with her sister, Merry, at Brimstone Buildings. I promised not to tell anyone . . . but you can keep a secret, can't you?

Sure you can.

So listen . . . And remember, not a word to anyone!

2

1. Weava Charm

'I'm not coming to Witchmeet,' said Weava Charm. 'Who wants to go to a boring get-together for witches for a whole week?'

She waved her wand and a jam-jar lid spun into the air. It screwed itself onto a jar of black-magic jam. Weava smiled and sniffed the scent of blackberries, sugar and magic.

Weava's dad, Belfry, stared at his daughter. 'Weava, you *love* Witchmeet,' he said. 'And if you get into that school for bad fairies, this might be the last time we go together.'

'Witchmeet's no fun without Merry,' said Weava, dropping her wand. 'Everybody just talks about old times.' Merry was Weava's elder sister. She had left the village of Wandwood the year before to go to college.

'But what will you do instead of coming to Witchmeet?' asked Belfry.

'I'll stay with Merry at Wand College,' said Weava. 'I haven't seen her for ages.' She giggled. 'Merry is *so* bad and funny. Remember when she cast that bouncing-spell on the jam jars? They smashed everywhere, and she pretended she'd been trying to clean them!'

'Hmmm,' said Belfry.

'And when she pretended to lose her wand and did all her work *without magic* when she came back last holidays?' Weava sighed happily.

'Weava——' said Belfry.

'I'll take some of this jam and we'll make black-magic cake. I'm going to make one for the Head Hags when I get to the school. What's it called again? Hags' Abademy?'

'Weava!' said Belfry. 'I need to tell you something about Merry.'

'What?'

'Merry's not at college,' Belfry said. 'She's . . .' He sighed deeply. 'I should have told you this before. She's living in the city now.'

'With humans?' Weava giggled with delight. 'That's even better! We'll have fun.

I can help Merry bother humans!' She
clattered towards her bedroom in her
clunky shoes.

Her dad followed. 'Weava, you
shouldn't visit Merry just now,' he said.
'She's not herself.'

'Why not?' Weava pulled on her new
cloak. 'Where's my skull buckle?'

'Use your witchsight to find it,' said Belfry.★

'OK.' Weava reached down and patted her stocking. 'Dad, where's my wand?' She needed her wand to make her witchsight work. 'I must have dropped it after I used it to screw the lids on the jam jars,' she said.

Belfry shook his head. 'Weava, you *must* be more careful. You know the old saying: *Weak is the witch who has lost a wand; she's sure to sink if she falls in the pond.*'

Weava searched the kitchen. 'Maybe it slid across the floor,' she muttered. She bent down to feel under the cupboards. 'Ah, here it is.'

★*Witchsight is a special spell witches use when they lose something. It makes hidden things easier to find.*

She pulled out the wand and shook off the dust. 'But . . .' She stared at it in surprise. 'This isn't mine. It's Merry's! Oh, that's right. She had a new one for college.'

Weava found her skull buckle on the floor nearby, and used it to fasten her cloak. Then she spotted her own wand under the kitchen table and tucked it in her stocking. She thought for a moment, then added the old wand, too. She'd take it to Merry, for a surprise.

2. Merry

That night, Weava sat on her broomstick above the city. Lights twinkled through the streets.

Her sister lived somewhere down below. Weava pulled her wand out of her stocking. 'Find Merry,' she said, and used her witchsight. She closed her eyes, waved the wand and pointed it downwards.

When she opened her eyes again, her gaze was drawn to a tall block of flats.

'Here I come!' she whooped, and swooped in to land.

The sign on the block said *Brimstone Buildings*.

Weava tucked her broom under her arm and walked through the front door of the building. Still using witchsight, she climbed the stairs to Number 13. The door to the flat was open, so she walked straight in.

Her sister sat at the table, pasting pink labels on pink bottles and stacking them in a long box. Instead of her usual robes, she was wearing a dress with a full skirt and deep pockets.

'Merry!' yelled Weava, and dropped her broom. She raced towards her big sister and squeezed her in a bear hug.

Merry's eyes bulged. 'What—what
are *you* doing here?' she asked.

'I've come to stay with you. I've got
lots to tell——*ub-oof*!' Weava sneezed.
She screwed up her nose. 'Merry, what's
that horrible smell?'

'I don't know what you mean,' said
Merry in an odd high-pitched voice.

Weava sniffed. 'It's *those*.' She pointed
to the pink bottles.

'That's Candywaft perfume,' said
Merry. 'It comes in three scents: Meadow
Breeze, Mountain Spring and Forest
Bloom.'

Weava sneezed again. 'It's awful,' she
said, dabbing her eyes with her cloak.
'I suppose it's something you magicked
up to play tricks on humans!'

Merry's face went a funny colour.

'Weava . . . It's cool to see you, but it's really late at night for a visit. Is Dad coming to pick you up soon?'

'No,' said Weava. 'He's at Witchmeet. Let's put that stinky stuff outside.' She waved her wand and sang a little spell.

The box of bottles sailed through the air and disappeared out the front door.

Weava sniffed. 'That's better.'

'Weava, *no*!' cried Merry. 'You mustn't do silly tricks here!'

'It's only a shift-spell. Merry, look what I've got for you!' Weava reached inside her cloak and drew out a jar of black-magic jam and Merry's old wand. She put the jam on the table and held out the wand to her sister.

Merry took the wand and dropped it on the table. 'I don't want that.'

'But you could use it as a spare.

I thought I'd lost mine earlier and——'

'I don't need a spare wand. I don't need one at all. I got rid of my other one,' said Merry loudly. She put the wand in a drawer under a table in the lounge room.

'But, *Merry*! You've got to have a wand! You're a witch.'

Merry bit her lip. 'Listen, Weava. You are not to talk about witches or spells or brooms or wands around here. It makes you sound crazy.'

'Huh?' said Weava.

'It's nonsense,' said Merry. 'Can't you see that? I know Dad likes to play at magic, but it's silly and dangerous.' She chewed a fingernail. 'That's why I left stupid Wand College. I didn't belong there. I'm *much* happier in the city. I have this flat, and a job, selling Candywaft perfume. I even have human friends.'

'But——'

'I'm living in the real world,' said Merry. 'Not some silly magic game.'

'Magic isn't silly,' said Weava. 'I'm going to a school for bad fairies soon.'

'You're going *where*?' said Merry.

'It's called Hags' Abademy of Badness,' said Weava. 'I'm waiting for my invitation.'

'Don't be ridiculous!' said Merry. 'Of *course* you're not going to a school for bad fairies.' The clock struck eleven and Merry jumped. 'Oh dear, it's *so* late,' she said. 'I have to be at work early tomorrow. It's time you went home.'

'But I'm not going home,' said Weava. 'I'm staying with you.'

Merry started to protest. But then she stopped and stared at Weava. 'OK,' she said. 'You can stay. I'll arrange everything.'

'Arrange what?' asked Weava, puzzled.

'Everything,' said Merry. 'But now it's bedtime.'

She led the way into a tiny spare bedroom and closed the curtains, shutting out the night.

Then she gave Weava a hug, and said, 'Goodnight, Weava. It's lovely to see you again, in spite of everything.' She went out, closing the door behind her.

Weava took off her cloak and hat, and put them in a pile with her shoes. Then she climbed into bed in her purple petticoat, and slipped her wand under her pillow. She had an odd, empty feeling in her tummy and it wasn't just because she hadn't had any supper.

3. Weava Gets an Invitation

Weava lay in bed, worrying about Merry.

Why was Merry trying to live like a human? What was she doing, selling that silly smelly perfume?

Sighing, Weava rolled over. Eventually, she went to sleep.

A little later, she woke with a start. Something was scratching on the window.

Weava got out of bed and opened the curtains, but all she saw was her own reflection.

She opened the window and something sprang into the room. The thing landed on her pillow and gave itself a few licks. It looked like a small black kitten, about the size of Weava's hand. It had furry wings and silver claws to match its eyes.

'Do you know what *I* am, witchling?' the thing said.

'You're a critter-fae,' said Weava.

'Correct. I am the kit-fae. I'm the only one of my kind,' the creature said. 'The hags sent me to Witchmeet to find you, but you never turned up.' It sniffed. 'I had to use critter-fae-sight to find you. What are you doing here?'

'I came to see my sister, Merry,' said

Weava. 'But she's changed. She's stopped doing magic.' A tear trickled down her cheek.

'This might cheer you up!' said the kit-fae. From somewhere in its fur it produced a piece of parchment.

Weava stared. 'Is that my invitation?' She wiped her eyes on her petticoat. '*Oooh!* You mean I'm going to the Abademy?' She danced around the room in glee.

'Not so fast,' said the kit-fae. 'You haven't earned a place there, yet. Read the invitation.'

Weava took the invitation and read the words aloud. '*Are* **you** *a* **wilful witch?** *Do you relish being* **truly troublesome,** **dreadfully disobedient** *and* **mindbogglingly** **bad?** *Answer Yes or No.*'

Weava beamed at the kit-fae. 'Yes!' she said.

More lines appeared. '*If you answered Yes, you may earn a Badge of Badness and attend the Hags' Abademy for further badness training.*' Weava danced around the room again.

'Keep reading,' said the kit–fae.

'*To qualify for your badge, you must create and perform a new and original act of breathtaking badness. Answer I Will or I Won't,'* Weava read. 'I will!' she said.

More words appeared, and Weava read them out. *'You have made a wise decision. The kit-fae will guide you.'*

Weava twirled around in her petticoat. 'I have an invitation to apply for a Badge of Badness!' she whispered. 'I'm going to the Abademy!'

The kit-fae twitched its fluffy black tail. 'It sounds as though your sister will try to stop you,' it said. 'That will make your task much more difficult. Are you up to it?'

'I hope so,' said Weava.

'Not good enough,' said the kit-fae. 'Bad fairies have to be strong and certain.'

'I *can* do it,' said Weava. Then she sighed. 'I wish Merry was on my side. She used to be so much fun.'

'Witches who turn their backs on magic can never be truly happy,' warned the kit-fae.

'But I *want* Merry to be happy,' said Weava. She lifted her chin. 'I know! Changing Merry back to her proper self can be part of my big bad deed! I'll do something *so* bad she'll *have* to cast a spell to put things right. That will remind her she's a witch, once and for all.'

4. Weava Makes a Cake

Early the next morning, Merry tapped on
Weava's bedroom door. 'Good morning!'
she trilled.

'Stop *trilling*,' said Weava. 'It makes you
sound like a good fairy.'

Merry smiled. 'Up you get! I've
cancelled work today so I can keep an eye
on you. And guess what? A girl called
Jemima lives in the flat next door to us.

I'm sure the two of you will be friends.'

'Is she a human?' asked Weava.

'What else could she be?'

'Fairy-breed,' said Weava. 'Like you, and me.'

'Don't be silly,' said Merry. 'Fairy-breed are banned from the flat. We're both living like humans now.' She left the room.

Weava got out of bed. 'Where are my clothes?' she said.

'Your sister stole them,' said the kit-fae. It crawled out of the blankets. 'She wants you to wear human clothes.'

It nodded towards a pair of shorts and a T-shirt where Weava's things had been. 'She's got a plan to make you live like her.'

'I've got a plan, too!' said Weava. She grabbed her wand from under her pillow and marched into the lounge room, still wearing her petticoat. 'Give me my clothes,' she said to Merry.

'You're too old for playing dress-ups,' said Merry. 'Have some toast.'

Weava held out her hand. 'I want my clothes.'

'I put some proper clothes out for you.'

Weava waved her wand and chanted a truth-tell-spell.

Merry flinched as the spell hit her in the face.

'Where are my clothes?' Weava asked again.

'I packed them up to give to my neighbour, Mrs James, for her costume parties——' Merry clapped her hand over her mouth.

Weava cast a come-to-me-spell. Her clothes flew out of a box by the door and landed on the table.

Merry's phone rang. She walked over and picked it up. 'Mary Charm speaking,' she said. 'Today? But I thought . . .' She paused, and listened to the person speaking on the other end. 'OK. I'll bring the Candywaft perfume delivery now,' she said, and hung up.

Weava put on her old clothes. 'I'm wearing these,' she said.

Her sister threw up her hands. 'All *right*! I haven't got time to argue. I have to go to work after all.'

Weava noticed the box of pink bottles was back on the table.

'I'll come back at lunchtime,' said Merry. 'I can't force you to stay in the flat——'

'Yes, you can,' said Weava. 'Just pick up your wand and cast a stick–tight–spell at me.'

Merry went pink. She strode over to
Weava and snatched the wand out of
her hand. Then she stuffed it into one
of her dress pockets and headed for the
door. Weava was about to yell at her,
when she saw the kit-fae flitting behind
her sister. It seized Weava's wand from
Merry's pocket without her noticing.
Then it darted back to Weava's bedroom.

'Oh, I almost forgot!' said Merry. She turned back and went to the lounge-room table. She pulled out a drawer and removed the wand she had put there last night. This she stuffed into her other skirt pocket.

She hoisted the box of perfume and staggered out the door. 'Stay here!' she yelled over her shoulder.

'Huh,' said Weava. 'A fly-me-spell would be much easier. The box would float next to her while she walked.'

'Very silly,' agreed the kit-fae. Now Merry had gone, it slunk out of Weava's bedroom, gripping Weava's wand in its mouth. It spat it out onto the table, and sneezed.

Weava helped herself to a slice of toast. Now, where had Merry put that jar of black-magic jam? She cast a spell and found the jar in the kitchen rubbish bin. Merry had thrown it away.

Weava was insulted. 'I made that!' she said.

'Your sister has human friends,' said the kit-fae. It giggled. 'Do you know what happens when humans eat witch food? They love it so much, they eat until they get tummy aches.'

Weava grinned. 'Right!' she said. 'I'll make a black-magic jam cake and give some to that human girl Merry wants me to play with. That can be the beginning of my bad deed. Merry will *have* to do a spell to fix the girl's tummy ache.'

Weava found the ingredients for a cake in the pantry. She dumped flour in a basin and used her wand to beat it up with eggs and milk.

The kit-fae perched on the edge of the basin and purred happily.

Weava tipped the jam into the cake batter, mixed it well and poured it into a cake tin. Then she put the cake in the oven.

Two hours later, the cake, gleaming and purple as a blackberry, sat like a toad on Merry's best dainty plate.

Weava was admiring it when she heard Merry coming upstairs.

'*Yoo-hoo!* It's me!' called Merry.

The kit-fae swished its tail. 'I will not be *yoo-hoo*ed at,' it said. It flitted into Weava's bedroom.

Merry poked her head into the kitchen. '*Yoo-hoo!*' she said again.

'You sound like an owl,' said Weava.

Merry goggled at the cake. 'What is *that*?'

'You know what it is,' said Weava. 'It's a black–magic cake.'

Merry frowned. She put her hand in her dress pocket, but Weava's wand was no longer there. 'How did you get your wand back?'

'My friend took it,' said Weava. 'Didn't you, kit-fae?'

The fetch flew through back into the kitchen. 'Indeed I did,' it said.

'Weava!' said Merry. 'I said no fairy-breed in my flat! Don't break rules!'

'You did when you were my age.'

'Yes,' said Merry. 'And look what happened! Dad sent me to that stupid college and . . .' She trailed off. Then she shook her head, as if to clear it, and put her hand on Weava's shoulder. 'But everything is better now. And guess what? You can live with me from now on. Won't that be lovely? I'll send you to school and——'

'Oh, that's all arranged,' said Weava. 'My invitation to the Abademy came last night.'

'You're not going to the Abademy!' said Merry. She looked at the cake again. 'Get rid of this,' she said.

Weava cut a slice of the cake and put it in her mouth. '*Mmmmm*. It's scrumptious! Have some, Merry.' She cut another slice and pushed it at her sister.

Merry shook her head.

Weava licked her fingers. 'I'll share it with that Jemima girl from next door. She'll love it.'

'You can't!' gasped Merry. 'It'll make her sick. What would I say to her mother?'

'It doesn't make *me* sick,' said Weava. 'It's a wandiful cake.'

'Yes, but you're a w——' Merry closed her mouth. 'You're not giving Jemima that cake!' She grabbed the plate, tipped the cake into the sink and turned on the waste disposal. 'Go to your room, Weava!' she yelled above the noise.

Weava did as she was told. Frowning, she sat down on the bed.

What would it take to make Merry angry enough to cast a spell?

5. Jemima James

Jemima James was sulking on the stairs outside her flat. She hated Brimstone Buildings.

'Jem-*mime*-a!' her mother called.

When Jemima didn't answer, Mrs James came out of the flat, wearing a green wig and carrying a pink one. 'Cheer up, dear,' she said to Jemima, plopping the pink wig on her head.

'*Ugh*,' said Jemima, pushing off the wig.

'Come on, sweetie ... get into the party spirit,' said Mrs James.

'You're the one who likes parties, not me,' muttered Jemima.

'I wish you'd make an effort,' said her mother. 'I'm starting this children's party business for you. I want you to have lots of fun.'

Jemima sighed. '*I* don't think fancy-dress parties are fun,' she said.

'Nonsense!' Mrs James waved her hand. 'Guess what? Mary Charm's little sister is here for a visit. Her name's Wendy, I think. Now you'll have someone to play with.'

Jemima stayed sitting on the stairs after her mother had gone. 'Wendy Charm is a silly name,' she said aloud.

'I agree,' said a voice.

Jemima jumped as a girl appeared. She was Jemima's size, and she had curly hair. She wore a long black dress that came almost to her ankles. Under that were striped stockings and buckled shoes. She held a broom in her right hand.

'Where did you come from?' Jemima asked the girl.

'My sister's flat,' said the girl. 'I sneaked out when she wasn't looking.'

'Is your name Wendy?' said Jemima.

The girl frowned. 'It's *Weava*. Get it right. Names are important to witches.'

Jemima looked at Weava again. 'Why are you wearing a witch costume? Mum hasn't started her stupid dress-up children's parties yet.'

'I *am* a witch.'

'You are not,' said Jemima. 'There's no such thing.'

'I am so,' said the girl. 'Merry's one, too.'

'Who's Merry? Do you mean *Mary* from next door?'

'Yes, she's my sister. But her name's not Mary.' The girl sat down beside Jemima. 'That woman with the green hair got her name wrong, too.'

'That's my mum,' said Jemima. 'How do you know what she said? You weren't here.'

'I *was* here,' said Weava. 'You just didn't see me.'

'But——' Jemima began to protest. Suddenly, Weava wasn't there any more.

'Weava?' Jemima glanced up and down the stairs. 'Where did you go?'

'Nowhere,' said Weava's voice, out of thin air.

Jemima blinked. There Weava was again, sitting on a stair. 'You're a ghost?'

'A witch,' said Weava. 'I didn't go anywhere. I just put on my DNM spell so you couldn't see me.'*

'Witches aren't real,' said Jemima.

Weava smiled. 'Yes, they are. I'll prove it to you. Let's go to my room.'

Jemima got up off the stair. 'OK.'

Weava got on her broom, and patted the stick behind her. 'Jump on!' she said.

Jemima got on and put her arms around Weava. Weava whispered something, and the broom lifted into the air and glided down the stairs.

Jemima gasped. 'I thought we were going to your room!'

'We are. Through the outside window,' said Weava.

---

*Fairy-breed use special 'Don't Notice Me' spells to stop humans noticing them. They are called 'DNM's for short.

Jemima clung to Weava as the broom shot through the entrance hall, out the doors, and bounced into the air in the street outside.

'Duck!' said Weava.

Jemima ducked as the broom swept upwards, close to the back wall of Brimstone Buildings.

Then the broom swooped through a window and landed in a bedroom.

'This is my room,' said Weava. She sat on the bed and nodded to Jemima to sit down, too.

Jemima was glad to obey. Her insides felt as if she'd gone up in a lift very fast and then dropped back down again.

'See,' said Weava. 'I told you witches were——' She stopped short and stared at the foot of the bed.

'What?' said Jemima.

'Hush,' said Weava. 'No, no,' she said, still staring at nothing. 'This is part of my bad deed.' She paused. 'Yes, I'm sure. Take off your DNM spell, so I can introduce you.'

Jemima's eyes widened as a black kitten appeared on the foot of the bed. At least, it *looked* like a kitten, but it was spikier than any kitten should be. 'What's that thing?' she asked.

'I'm not a *thing*. I'm the kit-fae,' said the creature. It stretched two furry wings.

'*Uggg* . . .' said Jemima. 'It talks!'

'It's fairy-breed, like me,' said Weava. 'There are lots of us about.'

'Then how come I've never seen any before?' asked Jemima.

'That's 'cos we use DNM, or Don't Notice Me, spells to make sure you don't,' said Weava.

She frowned. 'Well, mostly. My sister isn't using hers now. She's living like a human. She wants me to do it, too. I'm trying to force her to do a spell so she'll *have* to stop pretending. But it's difficult.'

Jemima felt as if her brain was being stretched out of shape. 'Um . . . what kind of spell?' she asked.

'I was going to give you some black-magic cake, so you'd get a tummy ache,' said Weava. 'I thought Merry would do a spell to fix that, but instead she threw the cake away. She didn't need magic for that.'

'It was mean of you to hope I got a tummy ache!' said Jemima. 'I've never done anything bad to you!'

'That's the point,' said Weava. 'I have to do something really naughty, otherwise Merry will ignore it. Besides—I must do a bad deed so I can win my Badge of Badness. I can't get into the Abademy without it.' She smiled at Jemima. 'The Abademy of Badness is a special school for fairy-breed. Once I'm there, I'll be happy.'

'I'd be happy, too, if Mum would stop trying to *make* me have fun,' said Jemima.

'I wish she'd listen when I tell her I don't *want* to go to costume parties.'

'Your mum and my sister should stop meddling,' said Weava. 'Maybe you could help me teach my sister a lesson, and I'll do the same with your mum?'

'It's a deal,' said Jemima.

6. Battle for the Broomstick

'I've thought of a *wandiful* bad deed, Jemima,' said Weava. 'It will teach your mother a lesson, *and* force Merry to do something witchy.'

She jumped off the bed. 'Broomstick time! We'll ride around this building and in and out of the windows. *Everyone* will see us. Your mother will be scared, and Merry will *have* to do a spell to get us down. Then she'll do a forgettery-spell on everyone who saw us.'*

The kit-fae was delighted. 'Now you're talking, witchling!' it yowled. 'That's big. That's bad. The hags love a grand performance.'

Weava took her broom in one hand. 'You come, too,' she said to the kit-fae. It sprang up and crawled under her cloak. 'Come on,' she said to Jemima.

They walked into the lounge room.

Merry was labelling bottles. 'Are you going to be good now?' she asked, without looking up.

'Of course not,' said Weava. 'Jemima and I are going for a broomstick ride.'

---

*The fairy-breed sometimes do forgettery-spells on humans when the humans have seen something they shouldn't.

Merry jumped up, goggling at Jemima. 'Where did you come from?'

'Through the window,' said Weava.

'Through the . . .' Merry's gaze shifted to the broom in Weava's hand. 'No!' she said. 'Weava, you can't take that broom outside. And take your costume off!'

'Give it up, Merry,' said Weava. 'Jemima knows you're a witch, and she thinks it's wandiful, don't you, Jemima?'

Jemima nodded.

Merry took Jemima's hand and drew her aside. 'Weava sometimes tells fibs. Don't encourage her.'

'I heard that!' said Weava. 'Come on, Jemima.' She tugged Jemima's other hand.

'No!' said Merry. She let go of Jemima and grabbed Weava's broom. She pulled hard. Weava pulled back.

Jemima backed away. She was

wondering if she should go home when someone banged on the front door.

Merry grabbed Weava's hand and pried the broom out of her fingers.

'*Yoo-hoo!*' Mrs James opened the door and put her head in. 'Mary, have you seen ...? Oh, *there* you are, Jemima!' she said. She came right into the flat, smiling. 'You must be *Wendy*,' she said to Weava. '*Love* the costume, sweetie.'

Merry began to sweep the floor with the broom. Her cheeks were bright pink.

'Hello, Mrs James,' she said. 'I expect you want your daughter.' She turned to Jemima and said, 'Off you go, dear.'

'Oh no,' said Mrs James. 'I only wondered where she was.' She strode across the flat and smiled at Weava. 'Maybe the girls would like to play witches in the park? It's a lovely day.'

'No way!' said Merry.

'Please don't shout,' said Mrs James.

'Sorry, but we're busy,' said Merry. 'My sister's about to tidy her room while I sweep the floors.' She pushed Weava into her room and shut the door.

Then she bustled her bewildered neighbours towards the front door. 'Goodbye,' she said.

'Just a minute!' Mrs James paused. 'I have an invitation for you.'

'An invitation?' Merry glanced at

Weava's closed bedroom door. 'What for?' she whispered.

'I'm throwing my first fancy-dress party this Friday. I'm inviting all the local children,' Mrs James said. She held out an envelope. 'Do bring Wendy.'

Merry took the invitation. Then she opened the front door.

Mrs James and Jemima went out.

Merry ripped the invitation into pieces and dropped it down the waste disposal.

*

In the spare bedroom, Weava sighed. 'Kit-fae, what can I do? Merry is so stubborn, and now she's got my broom.'

'Choose a new deed that doesn't involve your sister,' said the kit-fae.

Weava shook her head. 'No,' she said. 'Merry's a witch. I'll make her behave like one if it's the last thing I do.'

7. A New Idea

The next day, Merry made Weava come to work with her. 'Leave your wand behind,' she said.

Crossly, Weava put her wand on the mantelpiece. She was about to fetch the kit-fae from her room when Merry grabbed her shoulder and marched her out of the flat.

For hours, Merry drove a van from

house to house, delivering Candywaft perfume. Weava hated every minute of it. Her nose itched, and she didn't even have the kit-fae for company.

When they finally got home, Merry used Weava's broom to sweep the floor again. She wouldn't let Weava touch it.

'Why are you being so horrible?' asked Weava, taking her wand from the mantelpiece and sneaking it back into her stocking. 'I want you to be your real self again.'

'This *is* my real self,' said Merry.

She was still cleaning when Mrs James and Jemima came to the flat.

'Oh, hello, Wendy,' said Mrs James. 'Are you excited about the party?'

'What party?' said Weava.

'The big Halloween party on Friday! It's happening in the loft of this building.

All the neighbourhood boys and girls are coming. I gave Mary your invitation yesterday.'

Merry looked flustered. 'Oh . . . um . . . I must have mislaid it.'

'Never mind. I have a spare one,' Mrs James said. She took a card from her bag and handed it to Weava.

Weava looked at the words on the card.

'Halloween party this Friday afternoon!' she read. 'Come to the loft in Brimstone Buildings at 5 o'clock. Invite everyone!'

'You must come, dear,' Mrs James said. 'You already have the perfect costume. Where did you get it?'

'My dad made it,' said Weava.

'Well, you'll fit right in at my party,' said Mrs James. 'It will be such fun. You'll never see a party so full of ghosts and bats and black cats ... all the magic of childhood.'

Jemima moaned. She hated it when her mother talked like that.

Mrs James bent and pulled the wand from Weava's stocking. 'Oh, and what's this?' she asked.

'That's my wand,' said Weava.

'It's lovely,' said Mrs James, waggling the wand. *'Allakazam!'* she bellowed.

Then she laughed. 'You should see the ugly plastic things they sell in fancy-dress shops!' She handed the wand back to Weava. 'I'm sure you'd love to help Jemima with the party decorations, dear?'

Merry cleared her throat. 'Actually, Mrs James, my sister has a lot of—um—homework.'

'Oh, but it's the holidays!' said Mrs James. 'Every child deserves to have some fun in the holidays, Mary. That's why I started my children's party business.' She smiled. 'Off you go, girls.'

Weava grabbed Jemima's hand and scurried out the door before Merry could stop her.

'Mum's mean,' said Jemima, as she showed Weava into her flat. 'She keeps talking about *fun*, but look at these!' She pointed to a pile of black plastic bats.

'I've got to thread them on strings and take them all up to the loft. And then I have to spread out a whole lot of straw.' She sighed.

Weava had an idea. 'If I cast spells without Merry seeing, she won't know I've done a bad deed until it's too late,' she said. '*And* if your mother's party goes badly, that might stop her from having any more.'

'It *might*,' said Jemima. 'But what could make it go badly?'

Weava smiled. 'Having a real witchling there, for starters!'

8. Merry Snaps

Weava lifted her wand. 'Come to me, kit-fae!' she said.

The kit-fae appeared through the open window of Mrs James's flat. 'What?' it said, staring at the plastic bats.

'I have a bad idea for Mrs James's Halloween party,' said Weava.

'Weava's going to make the party go wrong,' said Jemima. 'It will be so bad,

Mum will never have another one.'

'And Merry will *have* to cast a spell to undo all the trouble I'm going to cause,' said Weava.

'That *is* a bad deed,' said the kit-fae.

Weava poked her wand in the pile of bats. 'Off you go to the loft,' she said.

To Jemima's delight, the plastic bats rose in a black cloud and flapped out of the flat and up the stairs. Weava, Jemima and the kit-fae followed.

The loft was huge. It was piled with pumpkins, hay, apples, cauldrons and wooden tubs. There were long tables, and cans of spray-on cobwebs.

'Right,' said Weava, 'let's get started.' She showed Jemima how to carve jack-o'-lanterns carefully. Then she waved her wand at the light bulbs, and flicked it at the plastic bats.

'Nothing's happening,' said Jemima.

'These are lie-in-wait-spells,' said Weava. 'It will all *look* normal until the party starts. I can't do right-now-spells. Your mother would notice too soon.'

'Oooh,' said Jemima. 'Can I have a sneak-peek at what will happen?'

Weava flicked her wand at the jack-o'-lanterns. 'Go!' she said.

The first jack-o'-lantern began to rock. Then it opened its slit of a mouth and gave a hollow laugh. 'Ho! Ho! Ho!' it chuckled. It rolled its empty eyes towards Jemima and started to jiggle.

Another lantern let out a spurt of smelly smoke and bobbed up and down. Shadowy little legs shot out and the lantern marched towards Jemima, pulling faces as it came.

Weava laughed as Jemima squealed and

jumped out of the way. 'See how scared
the kids will be at the party?' she said.

'Look out, witchling!' said the kit-fae.
'Your sister's coming!'

Weava froze.

The trapdoor to the loft burst open and
Merry appeared. 'Weava!' she snapped.

She stalked over to Weava and snatched the wand from her hand. 'I told you, *no more nonsense*!' she said in an odd tight voice. 'But you wouldn't listen, would you?'

Weava held her breath as Merry gripped the wand. Was Merry cross enough to do a spell?

But Merry continued, 'You just can't behave. Well, I'm going to stop your mischief. I should have done this the day you came.'

Breathing hard, Merry held the wand in both hands. Then she bent and snapped it over her knee, again and again.

She threw the bits on the floor and stalked out of the loft.

The jack-o'-lanterns fell with a soggy thud and lay still.

9. Where's That Wand?

Weava sat down. Two fat tears ran down her cheeks and she let out an angry sob.

Jemima swallowed. 'Can you mend your wand?' she asked.

'No,' said Weava.

The kit-fae fluttered to sit on Weava's shoulder. It rubbed its furry face on her chin. 'It's all right, witchling,' it said.

'It's not!' said Weava.

'Will the spells still work?' asked Jemima.

Weava shook her head. 'Not without my wand to set them off.'

'That's that, then,' said Jemima. She was so disappointed, she could barely speak, but she added, 'Never mind, Weava. You did your best.'

'I was trying to do my *worst*,' said Weava. 'Merry spoiled it.' Her chin wobbled and a tear ran down her nose. 'I'll never get to the Abademy now she's spoiled my big bad deed. And I've lost my wand, too.'

'Can you get a new one?' said Jemima. She handed Weava her handkerchief.

Weava blew her nose and thought for a moment. 'No,' she said slowly, 'but maybe I can get an *old* one.' She set off towards the door.

'Where are you going?' asked Jemima.

'I'm going to get Merry's old wand.
I brought it with me from home. All I
have to do is get it out of her pocket.'

*

Weava and the kit-fae spent the next two
days trying to steal Merry's wand, but
Merry was ready for them. She sewed a
button on her pocket, making it hard to
pick. And she wore her dress all the time,
even to bed.

But Merry didn't forbid Weava to go to
the party. She even organised the games.

'What's Merry up to?' Weava asked the
kit-fae at breakfast on Friday morning.

'She thinks she's won,' said the fetch,
nibbling on a rasher of bacon. 'She's
smashed your wand, so you can't do
spells. She thinks if you can't do spells,
there's nothing to worry about.'

'I wish I could get my hands on *her* wand,' said Weava. 'But there's no way to get it out of her pocket.'

'You'll have to try something else,' said the kit-fae.

'I do have one idea,' said Weava. 'I'm going to write some invitations and invite some friends to Mrs James's party.'

'Who?' asked the fetch.

'It's a surprise,' said Weava.

*

When Weava had written and delivered
all her invitations, she went looking
for Jemima. She found her in the loft,
blowing up black balloons.

'I didn't get Merry's wand,' Weava said,
'but everything's going to be all right.
Remember your mother said to invite
everybody? Well, I *have*.'

'Who's everybody?' asked Jemima.

Weava giggled. 'You'll see. Just don't
be scared when they arrive.' She climbed
out of the loft and down the stairs to
Number 13.

She arrived just as Merry dumped a
box of Candywaft bottles outside the
front door.

Merry smiled sweetly at Weava.
'Looking forward to the party?' she said.

Weava smiled back just as sweetly.
'Oh yes,' she said.

10. Party Time

'Party time, girls!' Mrs James called gaily, as she hung up strings of plastic spiders in the loft on Friday afternoon. 'Jemima, *do* put on a costume! I've bought you some lovely ones.'

'No,' said Jemima.

Mrs James threw up her hands in frustration. She was about to say something else when Merry climbed into the loft. 'Oh, hello, Mary!' she said. 'Give a goodie bag to every child. Remember, there's a prize for the best costume.'

Merry looked anxiously around the cluttered loft. 'Calm down,' she muttered to herself. 'These bats and cauldrons and witch hats are only pretend. The guests will be children in fancy dress. Weava, for once, will not look out of place. And nothing bad can happen at this party because Weava doesn't have a wand.'

'Here we go,' said Mrs James, as the clock struck five. On cue, the trapdoor creaked open and two little boys dressed as Dracula came in. Three girls in pink fairy costumes followed, and soon the room was crowded with children dressed as witches, ghosts, robots and fairies.

Mrs James soon had some of them bobbing for apples, while Merry handed

out goodie bags and organised games.

Spooky music played from Mrs James's sound system. Children yelled and laughed. The loft smelt of sweet food, face paints and straw.

Jemima backed into a corner. 'This is awful,' she complained to Weava. 'Mum's got that green wig on again! If only Merry hadn't broken your wand.'

'It will be all right,' said Weava.

'This is disgraceful, witchling,' the kit-fae said in Weava's ear. 'How dare these humans make fun of fairy-breed ways? That woman has a fake fruit drink in a witch's cauldron! It would serve her right if I turned it into a potion.'

'Remember the rules,' said Weava. '*I* have to do the bad deed, or I won't get my Badge of Badness and a place at the Abademy.'

The kit-fae sniffed. 'You'll have to think of something quickly,' it said. 'The hags won't wait forever.'

'It will be all right!' said Weava again. She really, *really* hoped that was true.

The clock struck six, and Weava crossed her fingers. She waited . . .

And then a cream cake flew out of nowhere and hit her in the face.

11. Hubbub

Weava wiped cream off her chin. 'Who threw that?' she asked.

The kit-fae went to investigate.

'There's a *troll* in that barrel,' it said when it returned. 'It says you invited it.'

Weava sighed happily. The invitations she had delivered had got into the right hands.

The troll grinned up at Weava as she

peeped into the barrel. 'Good party, witchling,' it said, and hurled a cake at a passing pixie.

'Thanks for the invitation,' said the pixie. She darted to where a little boy was bobbing for apples and dropped a snail down his shirt.

Weava saw three spooks drift through the skylights, and spotted some goblins eating apples in the corner. Under the long trestle table, she found nine small imps playing pass-the-parcel with a giggling lizard-fae.

Everywhere she looked, she saw fairy-breed.

'It's working!' she said to herself.

Jemima was passing by. 'What is?' she asked.

'My bad deed! I took invitations to all the places where the fairy-breed live.

Lots have come. They'll scare the humans and Merry will *have* to do something about it. Um . . . where *is* Merry?'

'She and Mum went to bring up more food for the party,' Jemima said. She looked around. 'Nobody looks scared to me,' she added.

'They will be once they see the goblins.' Weava pointed. 'See? There's one.'

'What, that boy dressed as a vampire?'

'No, the lumpy one at the table. And there's a troll behind that barrel.'

Jemima looked behind the barrel. 'No, there isn't.'

Suddenly, Weava realised what was wrong. She crawled under the table. 'Take your DNM spells off,' she said to the imps. 'Pass the word about.'

'*Oooh*, can we?' said the pixie girl who had spoken to Weava earlier. She squealed with delight and took off her DNM spell, then chased after two spooks. The message flashed around and all the fairy-breed removed their DNM spells.

Jemima stared as two trolls began a food fight. 'This is brilliant!' she said to Weava. 'Just wait until Mum notices! She'll never hold another party!'

She giggled as a goblin stuffed a whole pie into his mouth. 'Nice manners!' she said. Then she glanced up at the ceiling. 'Oh look . . . there's another kit-fae!' she said, pointing.

Weava looked up among the fairy lights. The kit-fae was perched beside a creature that looked like a cosy tabby cat with wings. As she watched, the tabby-fae flew to land by her feet.

'Hello, witchling,' it purred. 'I hear you are trying for a Badge of Badness.

It is an honour to be a part of your big bad deed.' It sauntered off, and rubbed its body around the legs of a little girl nearby. The girl stumbled and dropped her drink all over her costume.

'Thanks, tabby-fae,' said Weava.

A boggart jumped out of the apple-bobbing tub and splashed over to Weava. 'Grand party, witchling,' it said. Then it noticed a small boy staring at it. 'Boo!' the boggart roared.

The boy staggered back and sat in a sponge cake.

The boggart giggled until it rolled around on the floor.

All the children at the party began looking over their shoulders and backing away. Soon they were shuffling towards the door.

Just then, Mrs James arrived with a

tray of pumpkin pies. A troll barged up
and seized three pies.

Mrs James was knocked off balance.
'Careful, dear,' she said, trying to steady
the tray.

The troll grabbed more, and a spook
floated down to catch the crumbs.

Mrs James gasped. 'C–calm down,
children!' she cried, but the real children
were too frightened to listen and the
fairy-breed ignored her.

Weava danced through a cloud of bats.

The kit-fae turned somersaults in the
air. 'Brilliant, witchling!' it yowled. 'The
hags are bound to award you a Badge of
Badness for this!'

Weava spotted Merry at the entrance
to the loft. She ran over to her sister.
'Isn't this the best Halloween party ever?'
she said.

Merry went pale. 'But I broke your wand!' She patted her pocket with both hands. 'And mine is still in my pocket.'

'I know,' said Weava. 'I managed to make this party magic even *without* a wand.' She looked up. 'It's time you gave up trying to make me live like a human.'

Merry said nothing.

'Well?' said Weava, raising her voice above the hubbub.

'Weava . . . you don't know what you're doing!' Merry cried. 'Look at all these little monsters!' she moaned. 'And those trolls are letting off stink bombs!' she added as a dirty yellow cloud of smells rolled across the loft. 'Send them away, Weava!'

Weava folded her arms. 'If you don't like them, Merry, *you* send them away.'

'I can't!' cried Merry. 'They won't listen!'

'Well,' said Weava. 'You'll just have to get your wand out of your pocket.'

Merry went whiter than ever. She turned and dashed to the trapdoor and out of the loft. The next minute, a hideous noise clattered and yammered through the building.

The tabby-fae watched Merry leave. It blinked once, and then flew out of the skylight, away into the night.

'That noise is the fire alarm!' cried Jemima.

Merry returned and herded children down the ladder that led out of the loft. 'Hold hands and head to the entrance hall,' she said. 'Be careful. Don't run.'

'Whatever's going on?' asked Mrs James, swatting at a bat. 'What's that smell? Mary, did you sound the fire alarm?'

'Yes,' said Merry. 'Didn't you smell gas? It was so strong that it was making us see things. I think there might be a leak.'

'Nonsense!' said Mrs James. She gazed at the goblins. 'What are those rowdy children doing here? I don't recognise them.'

Merry didn't answer. Instead, she took Mrs James by the arm. 'The children were babbling about monsters!' she said. 'It *must* be gas.' Then she grabbed hold of Jemima with her free hand and steered Mrs James and her daughter downstairs. Mrs James protested all the way.

Brimstone Buildings emptied within minutes as people spilt out of the flats and down the stairs. Soon all the humans and most of the fairy-breed had left the loft.

'Where is everyone?' asked a goblin.

A troll launched another stink bomb. 'Them pixies and elves can't stand a good stink,' it said. Then it laughed and looked about. 'Well, there's no fun to be had now, witchling,' it added. 'No humans left to scare. Guess we'll be off.' It grinned at Weava and put on its DNM spell.

'I'm off, too,' said the goblin. It whistled shrilly and two more goblins and six boggarts grabbed fistfuls of cheese from the tables and clattered down the steps.

Weava and the kit-fae were the only ones left.

Weava's lip quivered. Her face crumpled and she began to cry. 'All that, and Merry *still* didn't do a spell,' she sobbed. 'It's no use. She's still acting like a human. I won't get my Badge of Badness, will I?'

The kit-fae looked at her sadly. 'I'm afraid not, witchling,' it said. 'But I can talk to the hags. Maybe they'll let you start again with a new bad deed.'

'No, they won't,' said Weava. 'I'll never get to the Abademy now. And I haven't got my sister back, either.'

12. Merry Explains

The fire brigade arrived, and big men in helmets and uniforms stormed up to the loft with fire extinguishers and hoses.

Parents flocked to the steps of Brimstone Buildings and left quickly with their nervous children.

Mrs James protested that a silly young woman had imagined a gas leak and panicked. No one listened to her.

Eventually, the fire chief returned. 'We couldn't detect smoke,' he said.

'I never said there was any,' said Mrs James. '*I* didn't sound the alarm. It was that stupid Mary Charm who wasted your time and spoiled my party.'

'There is a smell of gas, however,' said the chief. 'The person who sounded the alarm acted properly. *You* were the careless one for holding a party in a loft.'

'Oh, fiddle,' said Mrs James. 'We have a fire escape.' She tailed off and stared at the fire chief. 'I really like your uniforms! Is it possible to get them in child sizes? I think my next party will have a fireman theme! It can include a fire drill and . . .' Still babbling, she turned away.

Jemima sighed and clenched her fists. She went in search of Weava, and found her coming slowly down the stairs. 'What a mess!' she said.

'Yes,' said Weava. 'I won't get my Badge of Badness now.'

'Never mind that!' snapped Jemima. 'Mum's already planning another party. She's going to hire a fire truck next time. My ditzy mum is going to tell me fireman parties are *fun*. So much for helping me to change her!'

Weava sighed. 'If a bad deed like that didn't put your mum off parties, or make Merry cast a spell, nothing will.'

'You're a failure,' said Jemima, and trudged after her mother.

Weava was almost glad when Merry took her by the hand and led her silently up the stairs to Number 13.

'Aren't you going to yell at me again?' asked Weava.

Merry looked at her sadly. 'What's the point? Whatever I do or say, you just go on doing silly, dangerous things.'

'I needed to win my Badge of Badness,' said Weava. 'It's the only way I can get into the Abademy. And I really want to go there, Merry.' Her lip trembled. 'I've been so lonely since you left home. There are no other witches my age near Wandwood. Dad does his best, but a witchling shouldn't spend all her time with grown-ups.'

'I wish you'd forget about this Abademy,' said Merry. 'School is far less fun than you think.'

'But I want to be with bad fairies my own age,' said Weava. 'Don't you remember the fun we used to have when you got your spells wrong on purpose!'

'I got them wrong because I was no

good at magic,' said Merry. 'I *pretended*
I was doing it on purpose. I couldn't
pretend at Wand College, and everyone
laughed at me. Do you know what they
called me? *Messy Harm!* Once I turned a
tutor's cloak into cobwebs with a cleaning-
spell. Everyone laughed at me. I left as
soon as I could, and I decided I'd never
have anything to do with magic again.'

'So you're living like a human because your classmates made you sad?' said Weava. 'And you're scared the same thing will happen to me if I get into the Abademy?'

'That's right,' said Merry. 'I've been trying to save you from being as miserable as I was.' She gave Weava a kiss. 'Now, come and have some hot soup. Then you can go to bed.'

'I thought you were being silly,' said Weava. 'But really, you were just trying to protect me from being unhappy like you.'

'I don't want to think about it any more,' said Merry.

*

Weava was lying in bed with gloomy thoughts going round in her head when something scratched on the window.

Sadly, Weava opened the window for the kit-fae.

'I've come to say goodbye, witchling,' it said. 'You tried hard, but it didn't work out. I have to go back to the Abademy to report to the Head Hags. Now don't cry,' it added, as fresh tears dripped down Weava's face. 'You can't go to the Abademy, but I'm sure your dad will be pleased to see you back home.'

Weava tried to smile as the fetch flew away into the night, but she couldn't manage it.

13. I'm sorry

Someone banged on Merry's front door.
Weava reached the lounge room as Merry
opened the door. Mrs James pushed her
way into the flat.

'Oh, hello,' said Merry. 'I'm sorry your
party went wrong yesterday.'

'Sorry!' said Mrs James. 'Thanks to
you, I might lose my job, and you're
sorry?' She glared at Merry. 'The landlord

has just been to see me and do you know what? He says I can't hold any more parties in the loft!'

'But I only sounded the fire alarm,' said Merry. 'And the fire chief agreed the loft smelt of gas.'

'You sounded the fire alarm because you *thought* you smelt a leak!' said Mrs James. 'What was wrong with mentioning it to me, quietly? We could have held a costume parade down the stairs and *then* called the experts. But no, you had to cause a panic.'

'I'm sorry,' said Merry again.

'You make everything into a drama!' said Mrs James. 'And the way you bully that poor little sister of yours . . . it's no wonder she's such a little weirdo.'

'I'm sorry,' said Merry a third time. She sounded as if she was about to cry.

'Jemima says you *broke* your sister's toy wand on purpose! You're not fit——'

Weava pushed past Merry. 'Stop being horrible to Merry!' she said. '*I* invited the guests who ruined your party and made the gas smells,' said Weava. 'So don't blame Merry!'

Mrs James stared at Weava. '*You* invited those thugs?' she said. 'Well, now I see why Jemima's fed up with you. We've been nothing but nice to you, and *this* is how you repay us? You're a brat!'

'That's enough,' said Merry quietly. She put her hands on Weava's shoulders and pushed her gently towards the front door. 'Why don't you find Jemima and make friends with her again, Weava?'

'I'm not having that little witch near my child!' snapped Mrs James.

Just then, Weava spotted Jemima standing outside Merry's front door. Jemima was looking horrified.

'I'm going to tell all the neighbours what I think of your precious sister!' Mrs James said to Merry.

Merry stuck her hand in her pocket and pulled out her old wand. 'This is what I think of *you*, you old toad!' she said, and pointed the wand at Mrs James.

Mrs James vanished with a hiss and a cloud of green smoke.

14. Badge of Badness

'Mum!' Jemima squealed with horror. She ran into Merry's flat and across the lounge room as her mother vanished.

'Here she is,' said Weava. She batted the smoke away and picked up something small and brown.

'But that's a frog!'

'No, it's a toad,' said Weava. She held out the toad and it blinked at Jemima.

'But . . .' Jemima began to cry with fright. 'Oh, turn her back!'

'I didn't do it,' said Weava. 'Anyway, why do you want her turned back? Toads can't make you wear wigs, or hold parties, can they?'

Jemima stamped her foot. 'But she's my mum! The parties are horrible, but having a toad for a mum is worse.' She turned to Merry. 'Did you do this?'

Merry had dropped her wand. She was staring blankly at the toad. Her cheeks were white and her eyes bulged. She obviously wasn't going to answer, so Weava did it for her.

'Yes, she did it,' said Weava. She put her arm around her sister. 'But she wouldn't have done it if your mother hadn't yelled at me.'

Jemima's tears flowed faster. 'Mum's just ditzy. She yells when she's upset. She's sorry afterwards.'

Weava sighed. 'Don't cry, Jemima. Merry can undo the spell, if you want. Right, Merry?'

Merry swallowed.

'Please, turn her back into Mum!' begged Jemima.

'But I ...' Merry's voice sounded tight. 'I *can't.*'

'You can,' said Weava. 'It's like any spell.'

'It will go wrong. It always does!' said Merry.

There was silence, except for a sob from Jemima and a gulping sound from Mrs James. And then came a skirl of bagpipes echoing up the stairs.

'Now what?' moaned Merry.

Weava's mouth fell open with surprise.

The kit-fae flitted upstairs. Behind it, sailing up the stairs in a flutter of faded tartan, came three tall hags on brooms. Following them was the tabby-fae from the Halloween party.

'Morning, lassie!' said the first hag to Weava. 'I am Maggie Nabbie, and these are Auld Anni and Kirsty Breeks.'

'And you know me,' purred the tabby-fae.

Weava swallowed. 'I'm Weava Charm,' she said. 'This is my sister, Merry, and my friend, Jemima.' She held up the toad. 'This is Jemima's mother.'

'Aye, so I see,' said Maggie Nabbie. 'The tabby-fae said we might be needed here.'

'Have you come to tell me I've failed?' asked Weava.

Maggie admired the toad. 'But you haven't failed! This is a bonnie bad deed,' she said. 'Quite worthy of a Badge of Badness.' She glanced at the other hags, who nodded.

From among her tartan tatters, Maggie brought out a fat badge shaped like a jack-o'-lantern. 'Take it, lassie, and join us at the Abademy of Badness.'

Weava longed to take the badge, but she did not. 'I can't,' she said. 'I didn't do the toad-spell, and now I don't even have a wand. Merry did the spell.'

'She would never have done it if you hadn't come to stay,' said Kirsty Breeks.

'And a dastardly deed it is,' said Auld Anni. 'I've not seen a toadifying in *years*.' She smiled at Weava. 'Lassie, you've earned your Badge of Badness and your place at the Abademy.'

'So I did make Merry do a spell after all. I *have* done a bad deed,' said Weava.

Maggie offered the badge again. This
time, Weava took it. The kit-fae flitted to
Weava's shoulder and clung there, purring
with pleasure.

Weava pinned the badge to her dress,
and turned to her sister. 'I'm sure
I'll be happy at the Abademy, Merry,'
she said. 'I'll make lots of friends.

If anyone is horrible to me, the Head Hags will turn *them* into toads.'

'We will, too,' said Anni. 'We'll look after Weava. Now, Merry, will you allow us to take your wee sister to school?'

'I suppose so,' muttered Merry.

Anni conjured a new wand, and gave it to Weava. Then she cast a come-to-me-spell, which brought Weava's broom sailing from the cupboard where Merry had locked it.

Merry looked at the hags and managed a smile.

'What about Mum?' wailed Jemima.

'Och, yes, better turn her back,' said Anni. She raised her eyebrows at Merry.

'I can't,' said Merry.

'Yes, you can,' said Weava. She picked up Merry's wand and put it in her sister's hand. 'Just point it, and think about the toad changing into Mrs James,' she said.

Merry pointed the wand. 'Mrs James,' said Merry. 'I can't——' She broke off as the toad vanished and Mrs James appeared in a puff of smoke.

'Mum!' cheered Jemima.

Mrs James blinked at the hags. 'Have you come to complain about my party?'

'No,' said Maggie Nabbie quietly. 'But you should give up on parties.' She fished a battered book from her shawl. 'Take this pattern book and design stage costumes. You know you want to.'

Dazed, Mrs James took the book. 'Thanks very much,' she said. Then she opened it at the first page. 'What a lovely book,' she said. 'Jemima, come and look!'

Jemima peered at the book. 'Yes, Mum, it's cool,' she said. Then she turned and smiled at Weava. 'I'll miss you, Weava.

And I'll tell you something . . .' She came to whisper in Weava's ear. 'It's better to have a ditzy woman for a mum than a toad.'

'Maybe we could go for a coffee,' said Mrs James to Merry. 'I have so many new ideas I'd love to discuss.'

'I'd like to,' said Merry, 'but today I'm going to see my dad. I haven't seen him in a while and we have a lot to talk about.'

'Maybe next week then,' said Mrs James. She took Jemima's hand and led her back to their flat.

'And now it is time to take Weava to school,' said Maggie, when the humans had gone. 'Are you ready, lassie?'

'Almost,' said Weava.

'Then we'll be off,' said Anni. 'You follow.'

Weava turned her head and whispered to the kit-fae. 'Merry needs help with her magic.'

'Yes, she does,' said the fetch. 'That's why the tabby-fae is here.'

The tabby-fae leapt down from Maggie's broom. 'I've come to live with you, Merry,' it purred.

It rose to its hind legs and rubbed its whiskers against Merry's skirt. 'Don't worry. You'll like having me about the place,' it said. 'And I can help you get your spells right from now on.'

Merry looked surprised, and then she smiled. 'Thank you!' she said.

Weava hugged her sister. 'See you soon,' she said. Then she got on her broom and flew happily after the hags.

A Note from Tiffany Mandrake

Psst, this is me, Tiffany Mandrake, again.

Merry gave up selling Candywaft perfume.
Instead, she helps Mrs James with Stage
Magic, her new costume business. The tabby-fae
gives advice, and helps Merry with simple spells.
Stage Magic is doing well. The costumes look
good, feel good, and never need mending.
Merry often takes a weekend off and goes to
visit her dad.

Jemima is happy too, since her mum stopped forcing her to have fun. She still thinks of Weava and wonders: did she really fly on a broom? She looks forward to the day when Weava comes for another holiday at Brimstone Buildings.

And what about Weava? She and the kit-fae have the times of their lives at the Abademy of Badness with all the other young bad fairies. I live in a cosy, creepy cottage in the Abademy grounds. The hags know I'm here, and they trust me completely.

They know I'll never say a word . . . and I haven't . . .

. . . except to you.

About the Author

Bad behaviour is nothing new to Tiffany Mandrake—some of her best friends are Little Horrors! And all sorts of magical visitors come to her cosy, creepy cottage in the grounds of the Hags' Abademy.

Tiffany's favourite creature is the dragon who lives in her cupboard and heats water for her bath. She rather hopes the skunk-fae doesn't come to visit again, for obvious reasons.

About the Artist

Martin Chatterton once had a dog called Sam, who looked exactly like a cocker spaniel ... except she was much smaller and had wings. According to Martin, she even used to flutter around his head and say annoying things. Hmmm!

Martin has done so many bad deeds he is sure he deserves several Badges of Badness. 'Never trust a good person' is his motto.